YOU CAN'T EAT YOUR CHICKEN POX,
AMBER BROWN

PAULA DANZIGER

YOU CAN'T EAT YOUR CHICKEN POX,
AMBER BROWN

Interior illustrations by Tony Ross
Cover illustration by Jacqueline Rogers

A
LITTLE APPLE
PAPERBACK

SCHOLASTIC INC.
New York Toronto London Auckland Sydney

ISBN 0-590-50207-7

15 14   8 9/9 0 1/0

Printed in the U.S.A.   40

First Scholastic printing, January 1996

*To all my friends in Great Britain,
especially those at Heinemann and
Pan-Macmillan*

*with special thanks to a richness of editors, Gill
Evans, Vix Eldon and Margaret Frith . . . and to
Bruce Coville, who listened to this entire book on
transatlantic calls . . . London–Syracuse . . . and a
special acknowledgment to Scott Jackson, who actually said it . . . and to Carrie Danziger, whose
chicken pox started it all*

YOU CAN'T EAT YOUR CHICKEN POX,
AMBER BROWN

Chapter One

Third grade.

Here today.

Gone tomorrow.

I can hardly believe it.

It seems like just yesterday was the first day of school.

New pens, pencils, erasers, notebooks, clothes, a brain that had a chance to take a break over summer vacation . . . all of the things a kid needs to start a new school year.

Now it's the last day of school . . . just in time.

My pens are out of ink. My pencils are

1

stubs. My erasers are all erased. My clothes are getting too small and my brain needs to take a break over summer vacation.

It's definitely time for school to end.

"All right, class. Take a few more minutes to finish cleaning out your desks and then the party can begin," Mr. Cohen, our teacher, calls out.

Waving a six-inch rubber lizard in his hand, Mr. Cohen looks ready for vacation, too. Not only has he had to do all the regular

end-of-the-year teacher junk, but he's also had to do lots of extra stuff . . . because of what we all call THE POX PLAGUE.

For the last month, practically everyone in our class has come down with the chicken pox.

In class, people have either been absent or here and covered with scabs.

It got so bad that I even made up a sign to put on our door that says:

WELCOME TO SCAB CITY.

I, Amber Brown, have not been absent, have not gotten the chicken pox.

I am one healthy kid.

I never catch anything . . . . . except fireflies . . . . . and I let them go.

"Be finishing up," Mr. Cohen tells us.

I cram more of my stuff into my knapsack . . . my stick of lip gloss for when my lips get chapped (I only use it in the winter so it's gotten a little melted now that it's almost summer) . . . the good-luck troll that my

Aunt Pam sent to help me get through my math tests easily. I'm glad that she sent it but really nothing can help me get through math tests easily . . . except my best friend, Justin Daniels, who could explain it to me so that I understood it. But he moved away.

I pull out the large ball of used chewing gum that Justin and I collected.

He gave it to me when he left and I plan to keep it forever.

I've kept it in my desk because I knew it would be safe there and I haven't had to worry about my mom finding it and thinking that it's gross or something.

Next, I pull out a small photo album. I call it my "Dad Book." Now that my parents are separated, Mom doesn't really want pictures of him around the house. . . . I miss him a lot. He's so far away . . . in France . . . so I made up the "Dad Book" and keep it in my desk. There are pictures of my dad, alone and with me in them. There are even

a few pictures of Dad, Mom, and me together, pictures taken before they split up
this year, when we were all still happy . . . or
at least I thought that we were happy.

Keeping the top of the desk over my
head, I open the book to one of the pictures,
give it a fast kiss and whisper, "Hi, Dad.
Today's the last day of school. . . . I miss you
and can't wait to see you this summer."

"Boys, stop that." Mr. Cohen sounds annoyed.

I put the photos into my knapsack and check to see what's happening.

Jimmy Russell and Bobby Clifford are dueling with rulers.

They are so immature for people who will be fourth graders in only a few months.

They have scabs on their faces.

Personally, I think that each of them is nothing but a big ugly scab to begin with.

They always tease me, about everything, but especially about my name.

They always say things like "Amber Brown is not a crayon."

So I don't mind when they get yelled at.

I hear Jimmy whisper, "What's he going to do, flunk us? Grades are already turned in."

Obviously, Mr. Cohen has heard him, too, because he gives Jimmy a look and says, "It's never too late to change a grade."

The look does it.

Jimmy and Bobby throw lots of stuff in the garbage and quickly and quietly sit down.

Mr. Cohen is the best teacher in the world . . . or at least, the best teacher I've ever had . . . but when he gets mad he gets a look that is pretty scary.

I call it getting "cohened."

"Finish up, everyone," Mr. Cohen says.

All that's left in my desk are my bagel–shaped barrettes and my fuzz balls.

I take the barrettes and leave the fuzz balls.

Soon everyone is sitting down waiting for Mr. Cohen to speak.

I look around the classroom.

Half the people are out sick.

One, Freddie Romano, had to leave early because his dad's vacation time couldn't be changed.

Mr. Cohen makes a little speech about

how much he's enjoyed the year with us, how he's actually going to miss us, how even though we won't be in his class next year, he would love it if we visited him.

Then he hands out our "passports." All year long we used them to pretend that we were visiting different countries. "I want you to have these to always remember the journeys we have taken . . . to visit other countries . . . and the 'journey' each of you has taken to grow, to learn, to change."

I look at my passport.

All of the regular stuff is on it.

Mr. Cohen has stamped something new on it.

It says:

VISA——TO ENTER FOURTH GRADE.

And he's added a note to me:

"Amber—You've been a joy in my classroom. I love your sense of humor, your sense of exploration, your willingness to try new things, even when they are hard (like math . . . and like getting used to Justin's move).

You've used this passport well. Have a great time with your 'real' passport. Please send me some postcards. Have a great time in London and Paris."

I look up at Mr. Cohen and grin.

I will send him postcards, for I, Amber Brown, am going to London, England, with my Aunt Pam and then I'm going to Paris, France, to see my father.

It's a real trip, not a pretend one, and I can't wait for it to begin.

Chapter Two

First stop . . . London, England.

Amber Brown in London, England.

I like the way that sounds.

I wonder if I'll come back with an English accent.

I wonder if I'll meet any kings and queens when I visit their castles, and I wonder if they'll let me try on their crowns.

I wonder what it's going to be like to spend two weeks alone with my Aunt Pam in a foreign country.

I know that there is this amazing clock in London named Big Ben . . . and I wonder if there is also a Small Ben, a Medium Ben, and an Extra-Large Ben.

Second stop . . . Paris, France. I'll stay with my dad and Aunt Pam will stay with her friends.

I, Amber Brown, am one very excited kid.

"Amber, honey." My mother walks into my bedroom and puts a pile of clothes on the bed. "This is the last time we pack your duffel bag. I'm serious."

Flopping on my bed, she lies down next to my duffel bag, puts my baseball cap over her face and pretends to cry. "I'm going to miss you but it's great that you're going. I just wish I didn't have to spend the time before you go nagging about packing."

I decide to help her out. "Don't worry, Mom. You just lie there and I'll yell at me for you."

I pull the baseball cap off her face and then walk over to the mirror and say in my most grown-up voice, "Amber Brown, this is absolutely the last time you pack . . . absolutely . . . last . . . final . . . no more packing. You're driving your mother crazy. Pack. Unpack. Repack. . . . Three weeks ago your Aunt Pam calls and tells you about the trip. You hang up, run to your room. Pack. Then your father sends you some clothes from France. . . . You unpack . . . and repack. And you try to sneak extra things into your duffel bag . . . your stuffed

animals, your Monopoly® game, Tarzan the Ape, Rock and Rocky. Your own very tired mother has to go through the bag and take them all out. You pack. Unpack . . . and repack."

My mother's laughing.

Putting my hand on my hip, I keep staring at the mirror and continue to lecture myself. "Amber, this is no laughing matter. Look at the mess you've made. ENOUGH IS ENOUGH."

I stamp my foot and then turn to my mother. "Is that good enough? Did I leave anything out?"

"Good enough." She motions me over to get a hug.

I hopscotch over. "Pack. Unpack. Repack."

We hug.

The telephone rings.

I rush over and pick up the portable.

A man asks to speak to Sarah, my mother.

"Who is this?" I ask.

"Max," the man answers. "You must be Amber."

I turn to my mother. "Some guy named Max and he knows my name."

She smiles, then as she takes the phone out of the room, she starts talking to him in this very nice voice.

I hear her say, "I can't wait to see you either."

And I was so worried about her being lonely.

All of a sudden, I, Amber Brown, have a lot of questions.

"So, who's Max?" I ask when she comes back. I, Amber Brown, want answers.

"He's the brother of a friend of mine at work." She smiles. "He asked me out."

"A date." I gasp. "Didn't you tell him that you don't go out on dates? That you and Dad are just separated?"

"No." She sighs and brushes the hair out of my eyes. "Honey, I told Max that I will go out with him. Darling, you've got to accept that your dad and I are going to get a divorce. We haven't lived together for six months and we're never going to live together again. I think that it's time for me to start seeing other people. Don't you?"

"No." I plop down on the bed and pout. "I want you and Daddy to get back together again. I don't want you to go out with other guys. Are you going to marry this guy . . . make me live with lots of stepbrothers and –sisters . . . half brothers and sisters . . . ?"

"It's just a date." My mother laughs.

"I watch talk shows," I say. "I know what can happen."

My mother motions for me to stand up and come over to the duffel bag.

Then she hands me the two sweatshirts that my father sent from France, one of the Eiffel Tower and one from Euro Disney.

"It was nice of Daddy to send these so that I can wear them in London," I say, packing them. "He could have waited until I got to Paris. Then we would have had to buy more clothes here. See, Mom, he's being helpful, thinking about what we need."

She looks at me. "Amber. No matter what has happened between your father and me, I don't want you to ever forget that your father loves and misses you very much. I know that you miss him and that it's important for you to visit him."

She pauses for a minute, thinks and then repeats, ". . . visit him."

"I miss him a lot," I say. "Don't you?"

Quickly she shakes her head, and loudly says, "NO."

I can tell that my mother doesn't want to talk about my father anymore so I don't say more about him.

My mother closes the luggage, pulls a little combination lock out of her pocket and puts it on the bag.

"I don't know the combination." I tug at her sleeve.

"Exactly," she says. "That way you can't add one more thing to the bag."

We look at each other.

"Let's have some ice cream." She smiles.

"Chocolate chip with cookie dough?" I lick my lips.

She nods and then starts to hopscotch out of the room, saying, "Pack. Unpack. Re-pack."

I follow, doing the same thing.

Hopping, I think about how much I'm going to miss her even though I really want to go.

I wonder what's going to happen to her while I'm away.

I, Amber Brown, am going to talk to my dad.

Maybe he can move back and they can learn to love each other again.

Maybe.

Chapter Three

"Amberino, you've beaten me again." Aunt Pam holds up her Travel Yahtzee® scorecard. "Twenty-two games to three."

Amberino is Aunt Pam's special nickname for me.

Years ago I made her promise not to call me Amberino in front of the kids in my class.

We start Game #26.

I'm tired already and we haven't even gotten on the plane.

This morning I was so excited that I got up at 5:30 A.M. and the plane doesn't even leave until 7:00 at night.

After some last-minute shopping, we "dined" at McDonald's. One last vanilla milk shake and french fries before going over the ocean. Two weeks we'll be gone. . . . I slurped that shake to the bottom and wet my finger to get out every last bit of salt and french fry.

Saying goodbye to my mother, who was trying not to cry, was not easy.

She was so upset that I forgot to warn her

to watch out for bugs because I got a couple of bites while sleeping.

Once Aunt Pam and I went through the door and got our passports checked, I couldn't get out to see my mother again. Aunt Pam says that's what happens when you go to foreign countries.

So we've just been sitting around in the waiting area and playing Travel Yahtzee® games.

An announcement is made. "All people who need extra time to board should go now . . . also people with small children."

Aunt Pam motions me to follow her and the cart.

I, Amber Brown, am so embarrassed.

"Aunt Pam," I whisper, "I am NOT a small child."

She turns around. "I know. But you are young enough to board early . . . and, trust me, that's a very good thing to do."

We enter the plane and walk through an area with great big chairs.

"Can we sit here?" I ask, taking off my knapsack.

"In your dreams," Aunt Pam says. "This is first class, much too expensive for us."

My knapsack goes on again.

The flight attendants are giving out newspapers and drinks to the first-class passengers.

We go back farther and get to a section

where there are more seats . . . and the seats are a lot smaller.

"Here we are." Aunt Pam opens the storage space above our seats and puts in her carry-on bag. "You want to sit by the window, right?"

"Right." I jump into the seat, forgetting that I have my knapsack on.

Aunt Pam helps me take the pack off and we put it under the seat in front of me.

I, Amber Brown, am so excited.

This is my very first plane trip.

I look around.

A lot of people are in our section of the plane now.

Some of them are trying to stuff huge amounts of things in the overhead rack.

A guy is rubbing his head because he's been hit by a birdcage that someone dropped while trying to put it in the overhead rack.

Another person, holding her arm, got

hurt when someone walking past accidentally whammed her with an umbrella.

Pointing out the hurt people, I say to Aunt Pam, "Now I know why you want to get on early."

"Trust me. I've been going to London at least once a year for the last fifteen years. When it comes to traveling, I know what to do."

She pats the top of my head.

"I am not a dog." I hate to be patted on the head.

She smiles and says, "Oops. Sorry. But it could be worse. I could pat you on the head and call you 'Roverino.' "

Sometimes the people I love drive me crazy.

More and more people get on the plane. Some of them have so much stuff that soon there's no room in the luggage racks.

Finally, everyone is sitting down and everything gets put away.

I wonder what the flight attendant did with the empty birdcage.

I wonder if the bird who normally lives in that cage is flying over on his own and will meet the owner in London.

I wonder if the bird has got a passport.

I wonder if this plane is ever going to take off.

Putting on my seat belt, I realize that I'm so excited I can hardly stand it.

The pilot's voice comes over the loud-speaker and says that the plane is going to London, Heathrow Airport, and anyone not planning to go there had better get off right now.

A screen gets pulled down by the flight attendant and a movie explains all about safety and what to do if something happens.

That makes me nervous.

I look over at Aunt Pam, who is looking at a piece of paper.

"Pay attention, please." I tug at her sleeve. "You're the grown-up here."

She looks surprised and then she says, "Honey, I make this trip every summer. I know what to do. Don't worry."

The plane starts to move along the ground for a while and then it stands in a line of planes for a long time.

Just as I begin to think that we're never going to move, we do and the plane takes off.

It's so exciting.

I, Amber Brown, am up in the air.

Something tells me that this is going to be two weeks that I'll never forget.

Chapter Four

"Amberino, finish unpacking." Aunt Pam rushes me. "And then we'll shower, change, and take the tour bus."

I am so tired. Usually, as my mother says, I am "one very perky kiddo."

Right now, I'm too pooped to perk.

Flopping down on the bed, I plead, "Oh, please. Can't we take a nap first? Please, oh please. I'm so tired."

"Up, my dear." Aunt Pam tugs at my arm. "There's a five-hour time difference. Getting on schedule right away is a good idea."

There are reasons besides the five-hour

time difference why I'm tired. The plane left late. We ate, watched a movie and tried to sleep. Good movie. Bad food. Hard seat. Got served breakfast very early.

When we got off the plane, there was a long walk, a long line and a long time to get our passports checked at immigration, a long wait for the luggage, a long wait for a taxi cab and a long ride into the city.

Finally, we're in our "flat" (that's what apartments are called in England, Aunt Pam says).

Personally, I, Amber Brown, am one very tired traveler and would love to sleep on the living-room sofa bed.

"These two drawers are yours." Aunt Pam points to the bottom of the bureau in her bedroom. "I've unlocked your suitcase. Put your things in there."

Pulling out my clothes, I see that my mother has put in a few extra things, all wrapped up.

"May I open these?" I hold them up.

"Yes, you may . . . while I'm taking a shower."

She goes into the bathroom and I open the packages . . . three books, a jar of grape jam, a tiny troll ring, and English money to take Aunt Pam and me out for pizza.

Resting my head on a sofa cushion, I look at the presents.

The next thing I know is Aunt Pam is waking me up. "Honey, Shower Time. Don't sleep now or you'll never get on London time."

Stumbling into the bathroom, I try to keep my eyes open.

Finally, I get showered, dressed and ready . . . as ready as I, Amber Brown, can be.

Aunt Pam says, "Let's make a fast call to your parents to let them know that we've arrived. I promised them that we would call."

For a minute, I forget that we have to

make two calls, not one, that they aren't together anymore.

We call France first.

Aunt Pam says that way, with the five-hour time difference, we are giving Mom some extra time to sleep.

She dials my father at work, since it's an hour later in France.

I can't wait to talk to him.

Aunt Pam starts speaking to someone in French and then waits.

She looks at me and makes a face. "I hate being on hold. The only good thing about it right now is that the stuff that's taped to listen to while waiting is in French."

"Let me listen." I reach for the phone.

She hands it to me.

I don't understand one word. . . . But it sounds good.

I wonder if my father is going to have a French accent.

I wonder how much French I'm going to

learn while I'm with him. . . . I'll probably learn to say stuff in French like "I love you, Daddy," "Where's the bathroom?" and "Can we buy that?"

Maybe I'll learn enough to write a letter to Justin in French.

I bet nobody in his new school can do that.

There's a click on the phone and a voice says, in American, "Hello."

"Daddy," I yell.

"Amber." He sounds just like my dad, no

French accent. "I was in the conference room in the middle of a very important meeting . . . but I told them that we'd have to take a break . . . that my favorite person in the world, my little girl, was on the phone and in the next country."

"I can't wait to see you." I am so excited.

"Me too." He sounds as excited as I feel. "You're going to love all of the things that I've planned for us."

I'm grinning so much that it feels like my face is going to break.

He asks how the trip was.

I tell him.

In the background, I hear someone say something to him in French.

My father answers that person in French.

I try to understand what he is saying but I have no idea. Maybe he's saying, "Wait a minute," or "I want a tuna on rye," or "Jump in a lake. I'm busy. My wonderful daughter is on the phone."

He gets back to me. "Honey, the meeting is restarting in a few minutes. I've got to go but first let me speak to Aunt Pam."

I put her on the phone and they talk.

Then she hands the phone back to me and says, "Your dad wants to say goodbye."

I grab the phone and before he has a chance to say goodbye, I say, "Daddy. . . . Let's have a kissing contest."

"Honey, the meeting." He sighs and then he laughs. "Oh, O.K."

"On your mark. Get set. Go," I say.

We both start making fast kissing sounds for as long as we can.

My lips start to hurt.

"You win," he says, quitting.

I, Amber Brown, almost always win the phone kissing contests with my dad.

We've been having the contests since I was a real little kid.

"Honey, we have to hang up now but when you get here, we'll be able to spend all of our time together, no business. I've taken vacation days."

I can't wait.

We hang up.

I grin at Aunt Pam, who grins back. "Now we'll call your mother."

She dials and in a second says into the receiver, "Rise and shine, little sister."

She and Mom chat for a few minutes about the flight.

"Aunt." I stand in front of her and try to reach for the receiver.

She grins and hands the phone to me.

"Hi, Mom. . . . I miss you. . . ."

I tell her about the plane trip, all the waiting, everything. I thank her for the presents and start to tell her about what the apartment looks like.

Aunt Pam reminds us that this is a long-distance call, a very-long-distance call.

I hand the phone back to Aunt Pam, who listens to my mother for a minute and then says, "Everything's arranged."

Then I get to say goodbye, and Aunt Pam hangs up and looks at me. "Wagons Ho."

Chapter
Five

"Elevators Ho," I yell as we enter the elevator.

There are mirrors in it.

Aunt Pam looks really good. She's wearing a flowered sundress and carrying a really pretty sweater.

Her long blond hair is in one long braid.

And she has makeup on and this really pretty-smelling perfume.

On her feet are walking shoes.

Aunt Pam is ready to show me London.

I look in the mirror.

I'm wearing a long purple shirt. The shirt

is so long that it's hard to see the denim
shorts under them.

I've got sandals on.

My hair is just hanging there.

It was too tired to get put into ponytails
or anything.

I am not sure that I am ready for London.

In the elevator, Aunt Pam tells me that
elevators are called "lifts" in England.

She also tells me that the lines we waited
in are called "queues."

As we leave the building, I hear someone call out, "Pam, welcome back."

Aunt Pam turns and smiles. "Amber, I want to introduce you to Mary. She's the housekeeper here . . . and over the years has become a friend."

"Welcome to London, Amber. Is this your first time in our city?"

I smile and nod. "It's Amber's first day and we're off to see Trafalgar Square," Aunt Pam tells Mary as she takes my hand and walks up to the curb to get a cab. Even though I'm too big to hold hands anymore, I hold her hand. "Amber, do you remember what I told you about cars in this country?"

I'm so tired . . . and the cars are driving on the wrong side of the road, just like Aunt Pam told me.

I repeat her instructions, "Look both ways. Remember that the cars are on the wrong side of the road and look down at the sidewalk where it will either say 'Look right' or 'Look left.' You also said to be careful or I will turn into road pizza."

"Excellent." Aunt Pam gets us a cab. "We're on our way to Trafalgar Square, where the tour buses are."

There is so much to remember and I am so tired.

When we get into this great big black cab, I notice that the driver is sitting where passengers in America sit.

I wonder if they know that they've put the steering wheel in the wrong place.

I wonder how they drive when they go to other countries.

I wonder if I'm going to be able to sit in the car without screaming "Watch out."

Scratching at a bug bite on my arm, I think about how we really are in London.

The cab stops.

Trafalgar Square . . . here we are.

Chapter
Six

Trafalgar Square.

For a square, it looks pretty round to me, with fountains in the middle and a road running around it.

When Aunt Pam said that we'll be going to Piccadilly Circus, I was really excited, really looking forward to seeing clowns and elephants. Then Aunt Pam told me that, in England, circuses are circles.

We get on a bus.

I'm so glad that they call it a bus, too.

It's a great bus, a double-decker.

There's no roof on the top.

Rushing up to the top level, I get seats near the front.

Aunt Pam joins me. "Honey, put on your baseball cap, your sunglasses and suntan lotion. Don't forget that we promised your mom that we'd make up a scrapbook of this trip. Your camera, notepad and pen are in your knapsack."

I was hoping that she'd forgotten about the scrapbook.

"Tomorrow," Aunt Pam says, "we'll have a chance to see some places up close. Today we'll have an overview."

I scratch at my arm again. "And when we get back to the apartment, I mean flat, can we go to a drugstore and get some bug bite spray?"

She nods. "Remind me. Sometimes aunts forget."

I grin at her.

She grins back. "You know, I just love doing things with you. It's so nice when you come stay with me. And now, I'm really glad to show you London."

We sit in the bus, waiting for more passengers to get on.

A family gets on . . . a mother, a father and a little girl.

"Wouldn't it be fun if Mommy and Daddy were here, too?" I ask.

Aunt Pam takes off her sunglasses and looks as if she wants to say something about what I've just said.

I decide to talk before she has the chance to give me the LECTURE about how my parents love me very much . . . about how they just didn't love each other anymore . . . about how they're never going to get back together again. . . .

"Aunt Pam," I quickly say, "I really want to get a special souvenir for Justin. What do you think I should get him?"

She blinks and then thinks for a minute.

I wait to see if she's going to talk about

my parents or about the present for Justin.

Shrugging, she puts her sunglasses back on, smiles and says, "There are a zillion souvenir places around. I'm sure that we'll find him something wonderful."

The bus tour begins.

She kisses the top of my head and then takes the lens cap off my camera.

I take pictures of everything . . . Westminster Abbey . . . the Houses of Parliament . . . the Tower of London. . . .

It's so exciting.

I, Amber Brown, am seeing, in person, all of the things we studied in school.

We drive up to Buckingham Palace.

The guide tells us that it has a nickname, Buck House. He also tells us that the flag is not on the top of the palace because the Regent is not home.

I'm going to start doing that at my house. I'll fly my Yankees baseball pennant that I got when my father took me to a game.

I keep taking pictures.

There's so much to see.

I can't wait until tomorrow when we will actually be able to go into some of the places we're looking at now.

Some guy keeps standing in front of me just as I get ready to take a picture.

When my film gets developed, I bet that I'm going to have a lot of photos of the back of his head to put in my scrapbook.

The bus pulls back into its spot at Trafalgar Square.

"Off we go," Aunt Pam says, getting out of the bus.

"Nap Time?" I ask, scratching again. "Bug Spray Time?"

"Almost." She puts her hands over my eyes. "But first I want you to see something."

I can hardly wait.

Chapter
Seven

We haven't gone anywhere.

We're still at the fountain at Trafalgar Square.

There are people dangling their feet in the water.

I look at Aunt Pam.

She nods.

Taking off my sandals, I sit on the fountain ledge and put my feet in.

It feels great.

While Aunt Pam takes pictures, I dangle my feet and look around.

There are lots of buildings, an art museum, a church.

People are feeding the birds.

The birds are actually sitting on some of them.

I decide that's something I really want to do.

Taking my feet out of the fountain, I put on my sandals and rush over to Aunt Pam, who has just taken the eighty-seven thousandth picture of me.

"Please. Oh, please. I really want to feed the birds." I grab at Aunt Pam's sleeve.

"Amberino, if you keep pulling like that, one of my sleeves is going to end up much longer than the other."

I pull at her other sleeve. "Oh, please. Oh, please."

She takes some money out of her handbag. "Oh, all right. . . . Even though I think that these birds are vermin, rats with wings . . . it is part of the tourist experience. Go over and buy some birdseed and I'll take some pictures for your album."

Waiting in line, in the queue, I notice that my wet feet are a little squishy in my sandals.

I watch what other people are doing, putting some seed on the ground, on their arms, and in their hands.

I get the birdseed, go back to Aunt Pam, and do the same.

Immediately, one bird comes over and stands right at my feet. Then another bird comes over and sits on my arm. Then two more show up.

One stands on my head.

"Amber, I don't think this is a good

idea." Aunt Pam sounds nervous.

"I'm having the BEST time." I laugh as two more fly over.

I take out more birdseed and the birds eat right out of my hand.

Aunt Pam takes pictures.

When I run out of birdseed, the birds leave.

"Please, may I have some more money?" I ask.

"Are you sure?" Aunt Pam makes a face. "I'm afraid you're going to get some awful disease."

Pointing to everyone around me who is doing it, I say, "They all look healthy. Oh, please. Oh, please. This is so much fun."

She gives in and I get in line to get more seed.

While waiting, I look around and see a mother wiping some stuff out of her little girl's hair.

I hope that Aunt Pam doesn't see that.

I hope that no pigeon drops a load on my head.

Gross.

When I get back, Aunt Pam says, "Why don't you just put the seed on the ground and watch the birds?"

I bet she's seen the mother, the little girl and the pigeon poop.

I give her my "Please. Please. Please" look again and she gives in.

The birds return to me.

One in front. One eating out of my right hand. One eating out of my left. A couple of birds on my arms.

I just keep laughing.

Then one comes down, lands on my hair, and knocks off my baseball cap.

I don't mind.

Then that bird or another one quickly flies down and lands on my head.

I don't mind.

Then the bird gets his claws caught in my hair and tries to fly away with some of my hair still attached.

I do mind.

Aunt Pam rushes over and gets the bird off my head.

I can feel some of the strands of my hair ripping.

And the bird is gone.

In fact, all the birds are gone.

In fact, some of my hair is gone.

When I open my eyes, I notice that Aunt Pam looks a little pale.

"Can I buy more birdseed?" I ask.

"Not on your life," Aunt Pam says softly.

She really does look very pale.

Begging is not going to work this time.

"O.K." I hug her. "Aunt Pam, thanks. This has been one of the best days of my life."

She hugs back and then checks to make

sure that there are no bird gashes on my body.

"Showers," Aunt Pam informs me. "We're going home and take showers right away . . . and get you some bug spray."

At first I think she means New Jersey when she says home and then I realize she means the flat.

I could get used to living in lots of different places.

Chapter
Eight

"Amber Brown," I say to myself in the mirror, "you've either got pigeon pox or chicken pox."

They're not bug bites.

I kind of knew it but I kept hoping it wasn't happening.

Going back into the living room, I lie down on the sofa bed and try to figure out what to do next.

I miss my mother.

Aunt Pam is asleep in the bedroom.

I'm not sure that she's going to know what to do. After all, she's never been a mother.

My father is in France. He's never been a mother, either.

Some fathers are good when their kids get sick but my dad always just got nervous and let my mom take care of me when I got sick.

And I feel sick.

I itch.

A lot.

My eyes hurt.

My head hurts.

I'm having trouble swallowing.

I think I have chicken pox down my throat.

My entire body hurts.

I feel like I was run over by one of those wrong-side-of-the-road drivers and now I am road pizza.

I wonder if I'm just imagining things.

I wonder if it's the jet lag people always talk about, the time difference problem.

I don't think, though, that people with jet lag get spots all over their bodies.

I wonder if those pigeons did give me some terrible disease.

I wonder if there really is something called pigeon pox and if I'm going to die.

Here I am in London and I'm sick.

I wonder if there are doctors in England.

I wonder if my mother is going to have to fly over here immediately.

I wonder if my father is going to have to fly here immediately.

I wonder if my chicken pox will bring them together.

I wonder if I'm ever going to stop itching and feeling so rotten.

I look at my body again.

There are spots all over me.

Closing my eyes, I try to go back to sleep.

Maybe this is all a bad dream, a very bad dream.

No use. I can't sleep.

I open my eyes again.

It's no bad dream.

It's my worst nightmare, only I'm awake.

I want to scream.

So I do.

"Aunt Pam. . . . . HELP! ! ! ! ! ! !"

Chapter Nine

Dear Justin,
  I have chicken pox.
  Itch. Itch.
  Scratch, scratch.
  I have been stuck in this room for almost an entire week . . . a total tired week.
  Here's what Dr. Kelly said when she came to the flat. (Doctors in this country actually come to your house.)

  She said:

1. "Amber, you have chicken pox."
2. "There is no such thing as turkey pox."
3. "Put calamine lotion on every day."
4. "Don't scratch."
5. "You'll live."

And guess what else. . . . I thought that my mom and dad would immediately rush to my sick bed (actually the bed is fine. . . . I'm the one who is sick). And I thought that they would see each other and fall in love again.

Guess what. . . . that didn't happen. Dr. Kelly said that they didn't have to be here.

Aunt Pam said she could take care of me (and she has).

So my parents are not together. . . . boo hoo.

My itches have itches. . . . boo
hoo.

And I am getting sooooooooo
bored.

Please write back soon.

Your pal,

Amber Brown

I put the letter into an envelope and
look over at Aunt Pam who is reading a
book.

"Monopoly® Marathon," I call out.

"Amber." She looks up.

"Please," I beg.

She sighs.

I give her a pleading look. "My eyes
hurt too much to read . . . you don't
want me to watch too much television
. . . and I'm sick of counting my chicken
pox."

"Just let me finish this chapter," she
says.

I nod and smile.

While she finishes, I look at some of the chicken pox on my right arm and try to figure out what the picture would be if I tried to follow the spots.

I think that it would be a picture of a blob of throw up or of craters on the moon.

Aunt Pam sits down at the table where we've had the Monopoly® board set up for almost a week.

I throw the dice and land on Chance.

CHANCE

Go to Jail
Move directly to Jail
Do not pass "Go"
Do not collect £200

I feel like I'm already in jail.

Aunt Pam rolls the dice.

"Drat," Aunt Pam says. "I've just

landed on Mayfair. How much do I owe
you?"

"Two thousand pounds," I tell her on
our fourth day of "Marathon Monop-
oly®." "Or you can give me the deed to
Liverpool Street Station and the two
hundred pounds you got for passing
Go."

"Add the two thousand to my tab."
She sighs.

I look at the paper.

She owes 123,796. That's pounds, not
dollars. In England, they have pounds

and pence not dollars and cents.

The Monopoly® board is different but that hasn't stopped me.

I've got the best properties all in a row . . . Regent, Oxford and Bond Streets, Park Lane and Mayfair. (That's Pacific, North Carolina and Pennsylvania Avenues and Park Place and Boardwalk in the American game.)

I also own seven other properties.

Actually, being in Monopoly® jail isn't so bad, just sitting here, getting money and not having to think about landing on one of Aunt Pam's properties.

"Drat." Aunt Pam lands on Whitechapel Road. "How much this time?"

"Four hundred and fifty," I say. "But I'll let you get away with it this time."

"What a pal." Aunt Pam smiles at me. She looks tired.

She's stayed in with me the whole time.

Some of her friends visit, which is nice because they bring me presents.

Sometimes it's not so nice because I want her to pay attention just to me.

"Aunt Pam," I say. "Thanks."

"For what?" she asks.

"For everything."

She smiles. "Thanks for saying thanks."

I give her a kiss and then look down at the board. "You've landed on my property again but you can stay rent free again."

The phone rings.

It's my dad.

He calls every day.

And he's coming to visit me since I couldn't go there.

I hear about what he's doing.

I give him the daily Monopoly® report.

Then we have our kissing contest.

I let him win.

After we hang up, I turn to Aunt Pam. "Let's elevator race." I am so bored with just sitting around playing Monopoly®.

"Okey dokey." She's not only sick of playing Monopoly®, she's losing.

We get up and go out into the hall-way.

I go to the elevator at the other side of the hall.

She stays at the one near our flat.

"On your mark, get set, go," I yell.

We both push our elevator buttons at the same time.

My elevator arrives first.

I rush in and push the button for the ground floor.

In London, the ground floor is first and the first floor is on second.

I just know I'm going to win.

The elevator stops.

But the doors don't open.

I look at where it tells what floor it is.

It's between five and four.

I'm stuck.

I push the button.

I'm still stuck.

Aarg! I'm going to die.

I should have stayed in Monopoly®
jail.

I wonder how they will get me out,

how they will get food to me . . . what if
I'm not out by the time I have to go to
the bathroom?

Then I think about how I've never
heard of anyone dying by being stuck in
an elevator.

I'll just stay calm and wait.

Maybe they'll call one of those T.V.
rescue programs and I'll become a star.

"Amber." I can hear Aunt Pam yelling to me. "Honey, stay calm. Help is on its way."

I am calm.

Actually, this is the most exciting thing that's happened to me since I got the chicken pox.

Justin is going to be so jealous when he hears about this.

I do get just a little nervous when the elevator doesn't start up soon.

What if they don't get me out by the time I've got to go to the bathroom?

What if I miss dinner . . . and breakfast?

What if they can't get me out of here when my father comes and I'll only be able to hear his voice, not see him?

The elevator starts again.

It works and doesn't stop until it gets to the ground floor.

Drats! There are no T.V. cameras, but

Aunt Pam runs up and hugs me.

"Aunt Pam," I whisper, "I'm fine. Don't make a fuss."

Mary, the housekeeper, comes up to us. "When my son was a little boy, he got caught in a lift, too. And he cried and yelled," she says.

"He did?" I, Amber Brown, feel very brave.

She nods. "It was a very hot summer day. He was so warm that he kept taking off pieces of his clothing. By the time we got him out, all he was wearing was his knickers."

"Knickers are underpants," Aunt Pam explains.

We all laugh.

Suddenly, I'm not bored.

And tomorrow I'll really be able to see some of the places I've only been able to "visit" on the Monopoly® board.

Chapter Ten

Dear Amber,

    I just got your letter.

    Chicken pox, ha-ha-ha, what a turkey!!!!!(just kidding) I wish we still lived near each other.

    I'm going to karate camp soon.

    Remember in kindergarten when Vinnie Simmons had chicken pox and thought that the scabs on his arms looked like button candy... and how he was going to eat them until the teacher made him stop?

    Well... just remember... you can't eat your chicken pox, Amber Brown.

                your friend,
                Justin Daniels

I really miss Justin.

He makes me laugh.

Sometimes he also makes me want to throw up.

This letter makes me want to do both.

I don't know where I'm ever going to find another friend like Justin Daniels.

Aunt Pam quickly walks into the living room. "Sofa bed away."

We put it up.

Placing the cushions on the sofa, she says, "Amberino, are you feeling well enough to go out?"

"Absolutely." I grab my knapsack.

At the exact same time, we say "Wagons Ho."

We wait in the hall for the elevator, the "lift."

We take the elevator that didn't break down.

Mary waves to us as we leave.

It's raining a little.

Aunt Pam says that happens a lot in London.

We walk to the Tube.

That's what the subway is called in London. It's also called the Underground.

To make the trip even more interesting, I pretend that we are sardines in a can traveling to Sardinia.

I, Amber Brown, have a very active imagination.

We get off at our stop.

Aunt Pam says, "MOMI, Museum of the Moving Image, here we come."

And after a short walk we are there.

Aunt Pam says that we are at the South Bank.

I don't see a bank anywhere. Not south, not north, not east or west.

I'm confused.

"Do you need to change more American money into English money?"

She doesn't understand what I mean
until I say, "South BANK."

She laughs.

I hate it when people laugh when I'm
not trying to make them laugh.

"Oh, honey. South Bank is the name
of this area. It's called that because it's on
the south bank of the Thames River."
Aunt Pam is smiling. "It does get confus-
ing sometimes. Doesn't it?"

It sure does.

We enter, buy our tickets and go into MOMI . . . Museum of the Moving Image. It's all about the movies and television.

There are all these really old machines with pictures inside that twirl around.

In one of the rooms, we get to make our own moving pictures.

We sit down at a big round table, where there's a big hole in the center where the artist sits and shows us what to do.

He hands us a long strip of paper with twelve boxes in it.

I draw a stick person doing a cartwheel:

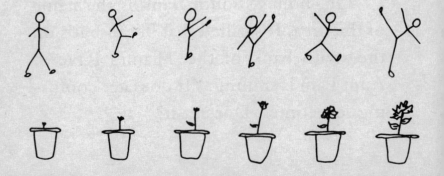

I, Amber Brown, am not a great artist. Neither is Aunt Pam.

Everyone sitting around the table puts their strips of papers in this machine that the artist calls a Zoetrope. (He says that means wheel of life.)

The machine looks like a hamster wheel with little see-through slits.

We spin our wheels around.

My stick person is not going to get a gold medal in gymnastics.

Aunt Pam's flower makes the machine look like the wheel of death.

I walk around and see what the other people have done.

My personal favorite is done by this kid who looks about my age.

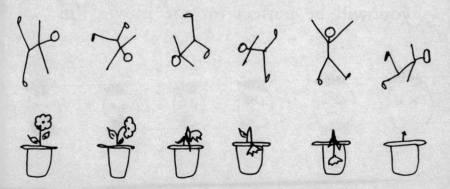

He's drawn a face that looks like it's puking. When you run the wheel backwards, it looks like the person is swallowing it back up.

It's really disgusting . . . and I like it a lot.

Justin would too.

"Wagons Ho," Aunt Pam says.

It's so embarrassing when she says that in public.

We go into "The Casting Office."

A guy dressed like an old-time director comes running up to me.

"Young lady, young lady," he calls out.

I look around.

"It's you. I want to see you. I think you will be perfect for the movie I'm directing." He tilts my head up. "Yes, perfect."

I wonder if he's directing a horror movie, "Scab Face from America."

He grabs a couple of other kids.

I become Lulubelle.

The boy who drew the puking face is Marv, "the meanest guy in town."

There is also Clint, the sheriff, and Ma Baker, the donut maker.

We rehearse for about a minute and then a man dressed as an old-time cameraman pretends to film us and everyone else applauds.

I could get used to this.

"Wagons Ho." Aunt Pam hands me my knapsack. "Wait until you see the rest of the museum. There's an area where you can pretend to be Superperson, flying over the City of London, one where you are a newscaster, and another where you are interviewed as if you're a big star."

I, Amber Brown, really like this . . . movies, television.

In fact, when we go back to the flat, I'm going to practice my name for someday when I become famous.

By the time I see my dad tomorrow, I'm going to be able to do my famous signature perfectly.

Chapter Eleven

Amber Brown

I've got my signature.

Now all I've got to do is get famous.

Aunt Pam comes into the living room, carrying her hair dryer.

There are no electrical outlets in the bathrooms.

In fact, they don't call it a bathroom. It's called a "loo." I wonder if people named

Lou hate that people call it that. I wonder if people in America named John hate that we call bathrooms "johns."

I'm glad they don't call them "ambers."

Names are so weird.

When I'm a grown-up, I'm going to have a COLOR party . . . and only invite people like me whose name is a color.

While Aunt Pam dries her hair, I make up my party list . . . . Brown, Black, White, Green, Greene, Redd, Grey, Scarlett, Violet, Rose, Amber. . . . I try to think of more names.

There's a knock on the door.

Maybe my father is early.

I rush to the door.

It's the porter, not my father.

"Letter for you, Amber." He smiles.

"Thank you." I take the letter. "See you later."

The letter is from my mother.

I rip it open.

Dear Amber,

We've been talking on the phone a lot since you've gotten sick, so there isn't much to say.

I was straightening up your room the other day. . . . I found a chewing gum ball. . . . Honey, it's really disgusting. But it is yours. We'll discuss it when you get home.

Don't feel too badly that you haven't had the chance to see London.

It sounds like you and Aunt Pam have gotten even closer. . . so it isn't all bad.

I hope that you and your father have a good time together.

Just remember . . . this is a visit. . . . you won't be going with your father to live in France.

I love you.

I can't wait to see you.

Love,

Mom

"Aunt Pam." I walk over to her. "Why is Mom talking about my not living in France? Does Dad want me to go live with him?"

She puts down her hair dryer and says, "May I see the letter?"

I hand it over and she reads it.

She looks sad.

"What's happening?"

"Your mom and dad are still working out the divorce. Amber, I don't want you to worry or think that it's going to happen to you. . . . Both of your parents love you and miss you when you're not with them. Your parents have discussed where the best place for you is right now and you should stay where you are. I guess your mother is just feeling a little nervous so far away."

"Wow." I am not sure of what else to say.

Aunt Pam hugs me.

"Amber, you have two very nice parents who love you. Don't worry. It's a shame that your dad had to go to France for his job. He didn't want to but he needed the job. . . ." She sighs. "They both just aren't very sure of each other. This divorce has been hard on both of them, but you can be sure that they both love you and never want to hurt you."

I think about how they have already hurt me . . . how my life is never going to be the same . . . not even if I can convince them to get back together.

There's a knock on the door.

It's my dad's special knock.

I, Amber Brown, am going to see my father for the first time in a very long time.

I have a lot to say to him.

Chapter Twelve

"Daddy, I love you." That's the first thing I have to say.

"I love you too." My father has his arms around me. "I've missed you so much, Amber."

We hug for a few minutes and we just stand there, looking at each other.

"You got taller," he says.

"And scabbier." I grin.

"You really did have the chicken pox." He grins back.

Aunt Pam comes over to us. "Hi, Phil."

"Pam." He reaches out and shakes her hand. "How are you?"

They always used to hug each other before my mom and dad got separated.

I guess Dad and Aunt Pam are getting a relative divorce.

"Fine." Aunt Pam looks at him. "Yes, Amber really did have chicken pox. Did you doubt us?"

I can't believe it.

My dad didn't think I had chicken pox.

Maybe I should have sent him a scab in the mail.

My parents are acting so weird.

I hate it.

"I wasn't sure." He looks at her. "At first I didn't think about it and then someone in my office said that his ex-wife used to tell him that his kids were sick and they really weren't."

"Mommy would never do that," I say. "Daddy, we talked to each other every day. You should have said something to me. I would have sent you a scab."

Both he and Aunt Pam laugh.

Actually, he laughs and Aunt Pam says, "Aaaarg."

Then my father gets a serious look on his face and says, "I just don't know anymore. . . . Amber. Let's not worry about things today. Let's just have a lot of fun."

Well, I, Amber Brown, know. And I

need to let him know what I feel. Putting my hands on my hips, I say, "Aunt Pam doesn't lie. Mom doesn't lie. And you don't either. Right?"

He nods.

"And you're not going to take me away to live in France, are you?" I stare straight into his eyes. "Right?"

He looks shocked.

Then he looks angry. "No. I'm not."

"You weren't sure that I really had the chicken pox." I can't decide if I want to yell or cry. "So none of my relatives believes each other."

"Phil." Aunt Pam speaks softly.

My father and my aunt give each other the "not in front of the kid" look.

"Don't give each other that look." I stamp my foot. "This is all about me. It's my fault. If I hadn't been born, you and Mom could just never have seen each other again."

I want to run into my room and slam the door. But I don't even have my own room here to do that.

Maybe I should just fold myself up into the sofa bed and let everyone sit on me.

I flop down on the sofa.

I, Amber Brown, am one upset kid.

Why is everyone acting so different?

Why can't they all believe each other?

If they can't trust each other, how can I trust them?

I'm only a kid.

Why do I have to worry about all of this?

My father sits down beside me.

For a minute it looks like Aunt Pam is going to sit by my other side but she sits down at the table instead.

My father ruffles my hair. "Honey. Don't be so upset. We only have a few days together . . . and then I have to go back to work."

"I hate your job," I say. "Why do you have to go back while I'm here? And anyway, why did they make you move so far away?"

"Amber, honey. You know all of this already." He sighs. "I scheduled time off for when you were supposed to be in France. Then when you got sick I had to reschedule. And as for moving away, you know that I had to go to France for a special assignment."

"Did you HAVE to go? Or did you just want to go away because you and Mom got separated?" I want to know.

"I had to go."

I look at him.

He thinks for a minute and then says, "And maybe I didn't mind because it was a way to escape from having to deal with how bad everything had gotten."

"What about me?"

He says, "Amber, I've missed you so much. I can't stand not being around to watch you grow up . . . to talk to you all the time . . . to go to things at your school . . . to take you places."

"I miss that too." I start to cry. "And I miss just being a kid who doesn't have to think about all of this stuff."

He gives me a hug.

I hug back.

Then we look at each other and smile.

"Amber. I want you to know I've told my boss that when this assignment is finished I want to go back to the New York office so that I can be near you."

I clap my hands.

"Oh, Phil, will they let you?" Aunt Pam asks.

He sighs. "I hope so. And if not, I'll find another job back there."

"And you and Mommy will try to get back together?" I figure I should go for it.

He shakes his head.

"No. But your mother and I will have a talk and maybe work things out so that you won't have to worry so much."

"Will you really? Do you promise?" I want everything to work out, if not perfectly, at least better.

He nods. "It's a deal. I'll call your mother when I get back to France. Let's just enjoy our time together."

"O.K." I nod.

"Great." He stands up. "Let's go to Madame Tussaud's. And then we'll go to the

Hard Rock Cafe for lunch."

"Great." I stand up too.

I look over at Aunt Pam who is sitting quietly and smiling at both of us.

I look up at my dad.

He looks down at me and then over at my Aunt Pam.

"Pam." He smiles. "Would you like to join us?"

She looks at him as if to ask a question.

He says, "Really."

She smiles at both of us, nods and gets up. "Wagons Ho."

My father laughs and says to me, "She's still saying that, huh?"

I repeat, "She's still saying that, huh."

"Some things never change." He laughs, shakes his head and then bends down and gives me a hug and kiss.

I guess that some things never do change.

And sometimes that's good.

And sometimes it's not.

"Wagons Ho," the three of us say at the same time.

And we walk out the door.

Chapter Thirteen

Dear Mr. Cohen,

I'm sorry that I haven't written to you until now but there was nothing much to tell you. I was stuck in my room with chicken pox. . . . very boring . . . very itchy.

Now so much has happened that I'll tell you most of it when I get back to school.

Here's some of it now.

★ ★ ★

Madame Tussaud's is a wax museum filled with dummies (not dummies

like Jimmy Russell and Bobby
Clifford . . . but dummies that look
like real people) . . . I've put some
photos of me in here to show
you. . . . My favorite part was the
Chamber of Horrors . . . it was
scary and gross. I loved it!

* * *

The Changing of the Guard at
Buckingham Palace is not good for
short people like me. . . . I kept
getting hit in the head by tall
tourists carrying big camera bags. . . .

* * *

The Hard Rock Cafe is very

noisy . . . and has a lot of historical stuff like rock and roll things. . . . I think when I am a teenager I will like it more. There were a lot of people waiting in line to buy one of their tee shirts. (Not me . . . I sat down and got an iced tea which I dropped all over me so it was sort of like wearing a tea shirt. . . .)

★ ★ ★

We took a canal ride to London Zoo. I really like the big apes best (and I don't mean Jimmy Russell and Bobby Clifford).

★ ★ ★

Guess what? There are lots of McDonald's here. Did you know that in England, French fries are called chips (potato chips are called crisps). . . . weird, huh?

★   ★   ★

This is the longest letter I've ever written so I'm going to quit before my hand gets tired. . . . I have to write two more.

Your favorite student ever (ha!),

Amber Brown

P.S. I hope that you like my signature for when I get famous.

Dear Mom,

I love you very much.

I hope you had a good time on your date with what's-his-face . . . . but not too serious a time. (Don't

get angry at me for saying this . . .
but I think that maybe you . . . . .
and Daddy . . . . . . should take
marriage lessons if you ever decide
to marry anyone again. . . . Don't
feel bad because I say this. . . . I
think lots of parents need marriage
lessons . . . . and maybe even
divorce lessons.)

   Love from your daughter who
loves BOTH her parents very
much,

Amber

Dear Justin,
   I didn't eat my chicken pox.

LITTLE 🍎 APPLE®

Here are some of our favorite Little Apples.

Once you take a bite out of a Little Apple book—you'll want to read more!

Books for Kids with BIG Appetites!

☐ NA45899-X **Amber Brown Is Not a Crayon**
Paula Danziger $2.99

☐ NA42833-0 **Catwings** Ursula K. LeGuin $3.50

☐ NA42832-2 **Catwings Return** Ursula K. LeGuin $3.50

☐ NA41821-1 **Class Clown** Johanna Hurwitz $3.50

☐ NA42400-9 **Five True Horse Stories** Margaret Davidson $3.50

☐ NA42401-7 **Five True Dog Stories** Margaret Davidson $3.50

☐ NA43868-9 **The Haunting of Grade Three**
Grace Maccarone $3.50

☐ NA40966-2 **Rent a Third Grader** B.B. Hiller $3.50

☐ NA41944-7 **The Return of the Third Grade Ghost Hunters**
Grace Maccarone $2.99

☐ NA47463-4 **Second Grade Friends** Miriam Cohen $3.50

☐ NA45729-2 **Striped Ice Cream** Joan M. Lexau $3.50

Available wherever you buy books...or use the coupon below.

- -

SCHOLASTIC INC., P.O. Box 7502, 2931 East McCarty Street, Jefferson City, MO 65102

Please send me the books I have checked above. I am enclosing $ _____ (please add $2.00 to cover shipping and handling). Send check or money order—no cash or C.O.D.s please.

Name_____

Address_____

City_____ **State/Zip**_____

Please allow four to six weeks for delivery. Offer good in the U.S.A. only. Sorry, mail orders are not available to residents of Canada. Prices subject to change.   LAP198

Creepy, weird, wacky and funny things happen to the Bailey School Kids!™ Collect and read them all!

The Adventures of THE BAILEY SCHOOL KIDS®

TRIPLET TROUBLE

by Debbie Dadey and Martha Thornton Jones

Triple your fun with these hilarious adventures!

Alex, Ashley, and Adam

mean well, but whenever they get involved
with something, it only means one thing —

trouble!

○ BBT90728-X Triplet Trouble and the Cookie Contest $2.99
○ BBT58107-4 Triplet Trouble and the Field Day Disaster $2.99
○ BBT58106-6 Triplet Trouble and the Red Heart Race $2.99
○ BBT25473-1 Triplet Trouble and the Runaway Reindeer $2.99
○ BBT25472-3 Triplet Trouble and the Talent Show Mess $2.99

Send orders to:
Scholastic Inc., P.O. Box 7502, 2931 East McCarty Street, Jefferson City, MO 65102-7502

Please send me the books I have checked above. I am enclosing $_____ (please add $2.00 to cover shipping and handling). Send check or money order—no cash or C.O.D.s please.

Name_____Birthdate __/__/__

Address_____

City_____State _____Zip _____

Please allow four to six weeks for delivery. Offer good in the U.S.A. only. Sorry, mail orders are not available to residents of Canada. Prices subject to change.

TT4°